OAKLEY IN KNOTS™

STORY BY L. S. V. BAKER

PICTURES & ILLUSTRATIONS BY M. E. B. STOTTMANN

Published by

BAXTER'S CORNER
Books - Puppets - Art

"Oakley In Knots"

For information, address Baxter's Corner, P.O. Box 223, Harrods Creek, KY 40027.
www.BaxtersCorner.com

Library of Congress Control Number: 2012911873

ISBN 978-1-938647-06-2

First Printing, August 2012
V2.0

Dedicated to Baxter's Mom for her energy in helping launch our journey through her initial ideas to teach through art.

For most of us, shaking hands is quite easy.
Shaking hands doesn't make us
    feel nervous or queasy.
Oakley the Octopus has eight arms,
    more than plenty.
With eight arms and eight hands,
    his options are many!

Oakley's mother had taught him
    it is good manners to greet
with a shake of the hand each
    new person you meet:
a new friend, a new teacher,
    anyone new at a place.
Shake their hand.
    Say your name.
    Put a smile on your face!

Oakley was worried.
    Which hand should he use?
When shaking hands with new friends,
    which hand should he choose?
Would the kids at school laugh
    if Oakley forgot
which hand he should use and which
    hand he should not?

So Oakley asked Mom which hand
    he should use.
She told him there isn't a
    correct one to choose.
"It's not the hand that you use,
    but the shaking that counts.
Shaking hands is polite.
    You will figure it out!"

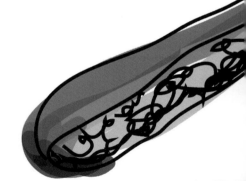

8

The next day at school
        the bell rang right on time.
As they entered the classroom,
        the kids formed a line.
Each student would stop
        before entering the room
to shake hands with the teacher,
        Mr. Marvin McBoom.

"Here it comes," Oakley thought.
        "It is time to shake hands.
Will I forget how to do it?
        Will Mr. McBoom understand?"
The more that he thought,
        the more nervous he grew.
So he decided in advance to use
        arm number two.

10

He held out arm number two
    as he walked through the door
just as Mr. McBoom reached
    for arm number four.
Oakley dropped number two
    and put hand four in the air;
but Mr. McBoom's hand
    was no longer there.

Oakley changed hands again.
    Mr. McBoom switched hands, too.
Their hands did not meet!
    That was sad, Oakley knew.
Out went arm number five,
    followed quickly by six,
then arms seven and eight.
    He was soon in a fix.

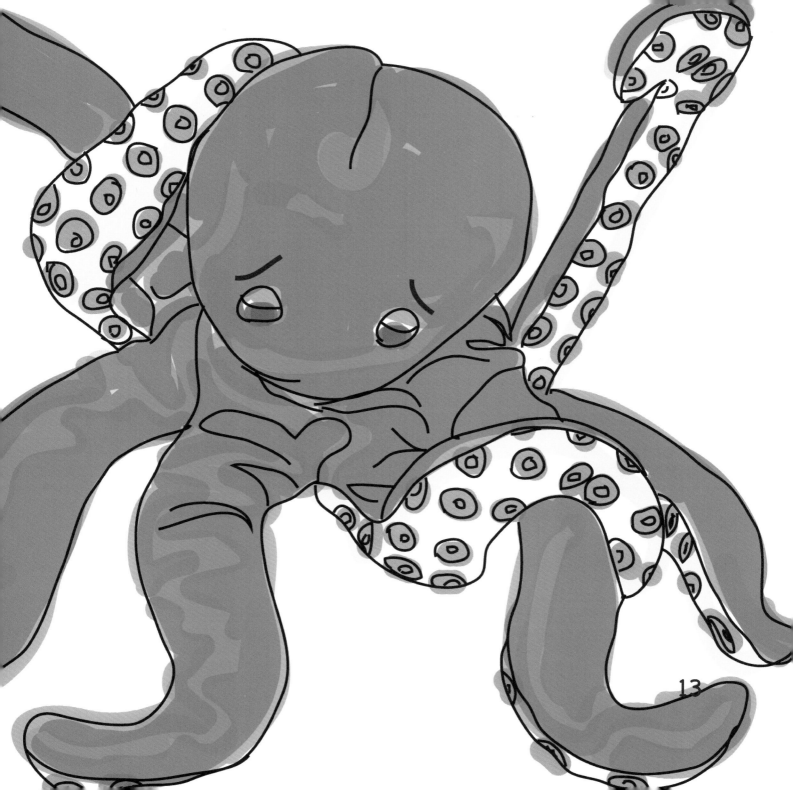

13

Oakley couldn't believe it!
     Because he forgot
which hand to use,
     he was now in a knot!
His classmates were laughing.
     Oakley's face turned bright red,
but Mr. McBoom calmed him down
     with a pat on the head.

"Young fellow, how marvelous!"
     said Mr. McBoom.
"I have one special job that
     needs eight arms, not two.
With so much to teach,
     I need to quickly clean boards
to make room for new lessons,
     new numbers, new words."

Oakley looked at the boards
    that were lining one wall.
Then he looked at his hands
    knotted up in a ball.
He thought, "Mr. McBoom believes
    I can do it.
I will just use the arm that feels right
    and get to it."

Slowly he loosened and pulled out
    arm number one.
With that arm unknotted,
    the job was begun.
He picked up one eraser
    and looked at the board.
He decided he should also use
    arm number four.

Without thinking it over,
    out came arm number three.
This really was easy,
    Oakley started to see.
He no longer thought
    about which hand to use.
He relaxed and unknotted.
    He did not have to choose.

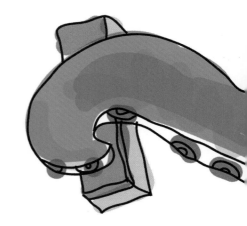

Oakley had figured out
    just what to do.
He grabbed ALL the erasers,
    and how the dust flew!
Oakley sailed down the boards.
    The kids couldn't believe
that their unknotted friend
    could move with such speed.

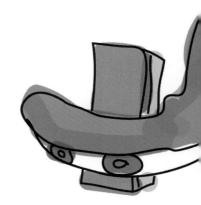

19

Oakley finished the job.
    He now felt quite calm.
He smiled as he dusted
    the chalk from each palm.
"I like having choices!
    I like getting to choose
which of my hands
    is the best one to use."

When the other kids realized
    just what Oakley could do
because he had eight arms
    instead of just two,
they clapped and they whistled.
    It truly was grand!
Now each one of them wanted to
    shake Oakley's hand.

The End

Building Character Is Child's Play™

Baxter's Corner provides a "Beyond the Story Book" experience using the story as the foundation that helps teach life's lessons and build character around social skills and fundamental values.

More than just a story, children are engaged through discussion questions and activities included in the books and online at www.BaxtersCorner.com. These activities extend and enrich a child's understanding of the differences and perspectives of others as they develop problem-solving skills and learn how to work together.

Our engaging animal characters wrestle with the same situations and choices that children face. Children will laugh at the predicaments of their new furry friends and find comfort in knowing others face the same challenges.

Along with innovative puppets and vibrant wall art, Baxter's Corner creates a rich environment for children to expand their understanding through play.

BEYOND THE STORY BOOK

Fun facts about octopuses:

• "Octo" means eight. An octopus has eight arms with suction cups that it uses to catch and hold its prey.

• Other ways to write the plural of octopus are octopi and octopodes.

• An octopus can regrow an arm that has been cut off.

• Octopuses have a large brain and are very intelligent.

• Octopuses live in the ocean, usually in coral reefs, where they live in the crevices. Some octopuses even pile up rocks and shells around their "home" as protection.

• Octopuses move through the water by crawling or swimming. They crawl by walking on their arms, usually on many at once.

• An octopus swims by expelling a jet of water through a muscular tube on its body called a siphon. It sucks water into the tube and blasts the water out to move forward, backward or sideways.

27

What do you think?

Search for specific examples from the story and illustrations to answer each question.

1. Why was Oakley nervous about shaking hands?

2. How do you introduce yourself to a new person?

3. What happened when Oakley went to shake hands with his teacher?

4. How did the other kids in the class feel about Oakley's dilemma?

5. Who helped Oakley overcome his nervousness?

6. What did he say that made Oakley rethink the situation?

7. By the end of the story, how do you think Oakley felt about shaking hands?

8. What activity influenced Oakley's attitude?

9. How did the attitude of Oakley's classmates change over the course of the story?

Do you have other questions about the story? We want to hear from you! Submit your questions to us online at www.BaxtersCorner.com, or email your question to AskTheAuthor@BaxtersCorner.com.

Can you find Oakley?

Find the answer on page 32

What other animals are in line with Oakley?

Find the answers on page 33

Oakley's friends

Left to right: elephant, lamb, tarantula, monkey, Oakley, red fox, monkey, bee, giraffe, frog, alligator, oyster, porcupine, and turtle.

Look at the illustration on page 31. Notice how animals are the same colors found in nature so that they blend in with their home environment of forest, grassland, jungle, pond or ocean.

If I met a Queen

What would you do if you
    met a Queen?
Would you stay perfectly calm
    or faint on the scene?
With good manners you won't worry
    about starting to mumble
when you meet someone new,
    whether important or humble.
Why, you'll be prepared to meet
    practically anyone.
It is not hard at all once you know
    how it's done.

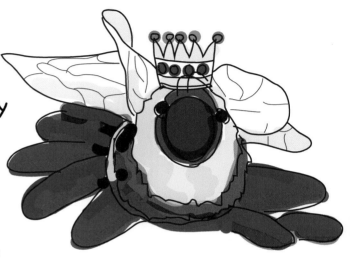

When meeting for the first time, introduce yourself and put your hand out...

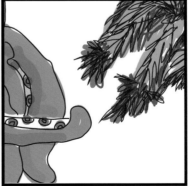

When I meet someone new

When you meet someone for the first time, it is polite to introduce yourself. Begin by saying hello, then say your name, shake hands and tell the other person something about yourself. Practice introducing yourself to a relative, neighbor or your teacher.

Mom, I want you to meet Tajo and his friend Mrs. Queen Bee. When he climbed up a tree, he met the Queen of the bee hive and they became friends.

Tajo and Mr. McBoom thought our class would enjoy meeting Mrs. Queen Bee to learn how honey is made.

Hello Tajo and Mrs. Queen Bee. I am so happy to meet you.

Hello Mrs. Mom and Oakley. Thank you for inviting us to visit.

Yes, thank you. I am particularly glad to be here because I am nervous about speaking to your class and would like to practice.

Oh. Now that I know how, I will introduce you to the class!

a Baxter story

Hot Dog Octopus

Turn a plain hot dog into a plate of fun!

Cook a hot dog and carefully slice in half from center to one end. Slice each of these halves into two sections each, to end up with eight arms. Cut small holes for the eyes.

Separate the slices and set the hot dog upright with the "legs" fanning out along with other food that would suggest the bottom of the ocean.

CAUTION: Parents will need to cook and cut the hot dog for young children and supervise carefully for those just learning to cook.

Word Play with Oakley

Rhyme Time

What words do you know that rhyme with these words? Find a word in the story that rhymes with each word.

face	forgot	use
wall	three	hand
greet	air	grew

Word Play with Oakley

Rhyme Time

Answers

face / place	forgot / knot	use / choose
wall / ball	three / see	hand / grand
greet / meet	air / there	grew / two

Word Play with Oakley

Short or Long?

Identify which of the following words have short vowel sounds and which have long vowel sounds.

hand	line	stop
right	kids	put
sad	job	fix

Find the answers on page 40

39

Word Play with Oakley

Short or Long?

Answers

⌣ Short vowel sound

— Long vowel sound

hănd   līne   stŏp

rīght   kĭds   pŭt

săd   jŏb   fĭx

Word Play with Oakley

Person, Place or Thing?

Decide whether each word is a character, place, action or thing.

shaking	ocean	Oakley	whistled
eraser	Mom	choose	reached
school	dusted	board	classroom
greet	arm	hand	Mr. McBoom

Find the answers on page 42

Word Play with Oakley

Person, Place or Thing?

Answers

Character = C
Action = A
Place = P
Thing = T

shaking = A	ocean = P	Oakley = C	whistled = A
eraser = T	Mom = C	choose = A	reached = A
school = P	dusted = A	board = T	classroom = P
greet = A	arm = T	hand = T	Mr. McBoom = C

Additional Resources

Visit Oakley's character page on www.BaxtersCorner.com for more animal facts and learning activities.

Octopus craft

Materials:

Paper towel tube
Construction paper
   (your choice of color)
Scissors
Glue
Crayons, markers, glitter, buttons,
   and other decorations

Instructions:

Cut a piece of construction paper large enough to cover the paper towel tube and glue in place.

When dry, use scissors to make a cut from one end of the tube to the center.

Continue making similar cuts around the bottom half of the tube until you have eight strips or "legs".

Fan out the legs so the tube is upright. Using crayons or markers, add eyes and a mouth. Decorate the body and legs of the octopus with designs, glitter, buttons or other items.

CAUTION: Parents will need to cut paper for younger children and supervise older children.

Other Baxter's Corner Books

Ally the Alligator Series

"No dad to coach soccer, to play games or read books. No dad to ride bikes or take fish off of hooks."

Tomorrow is Donuts with Dads Day at school. Ally the Alligator is not looking forward to this special event because she does not have a dad to invite. What will she tell everyone when she shows up alone? Everything turns around when Ally chooses to focus on what she has instead of what she is missing.

Ellema the Elephant Series

"Just imagine if your nose were as long as your arm. Sneezing with that nose might create an alarm."

With her long trunk, Ellema the Elephant causes quite a stir when she sneezes. When Ellema learns to control her sneezes, everything calms down. Perhaps things are too calm. Kite Day is nearly ruined when there is no wind ... until Ellema sneezes her biggest sneeze ever!

Fred the Frog Series

"Jumping," thought Fred, "looks like wonderful fun. I can't wait to grow legs and hop in the sun."

As a tadpole, Fred can't wait to jump just like the older frogs. But one of Fred's new legs is shorter than the other, and the jumping coach tells Fred that maybe jumping is not for him. Instead of giving up, Fred figures out a special way to jump. He practices and practices ... until he can hit the target every time.

CPSIA information can be obtained
at www.ICGtesting.com
Printed in the USA
LVIC05n0356060115
421464LV00002BA/4